On a Snowy Night

Jean Little

Illustrations by
Brian Deines

North Winds Press

An Imprint of Scholastic Canada Ltd.

The paintings for this book were created in oil on linen.
The type was set in 22 point Filosofia.

Library and Archives Canada Cataloguing in Publication

Little, Jean, 1932-

On a snowy night / by Jean Little ; illustrations by Brian Deines.

ISBN 978-1-4431-1359-5

I. Deines, Brian II. Title.

PS8523.I77O523 2013   jC813'.54   C2013-901805-0

6 5 4 3 2 1   Printed in Malaysia 108   13 14 15 16 17

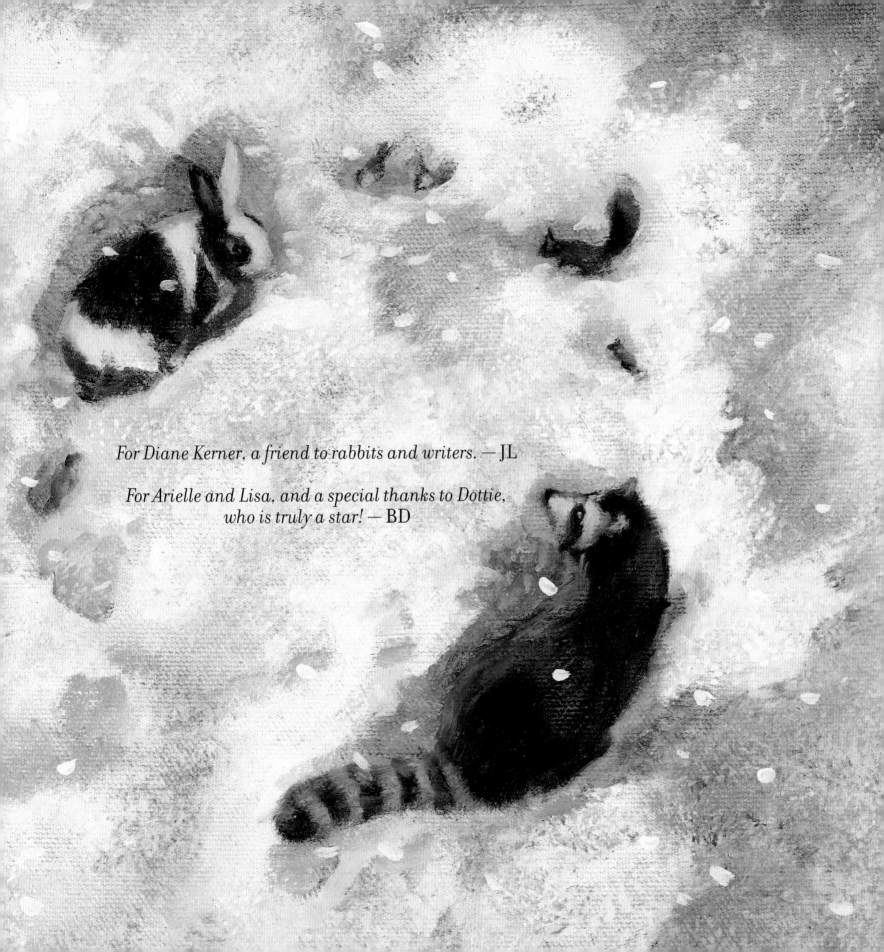

For Diane Kerner, a friend to rabbits and writers. — JL

For Arielle and Lisa, and a special thanks to Dottie,
who is truly a star! — BD

Rosa Rabbit wanted to bite somebody.

When Rosa was given to Brandon
on his fifth birthday, he had shouted,
"She's better than perfect, Mom!"

He stroked her and fed her bits of
carrots and apples from his fingers.
She nibbled, but she never once bit him.

"Who loves Rosa Rabbit?" he asked
her, but soon he would answer, "I do!"

And Rosa Rabbit was happy.

But now, Rosa was not happy at all. Brandon had grown big and he was too busy playing with boys to bother with a rabbit very often.

Rosa watched Brandon's sister showing her guinea pig the Christmas tree.

"Tonight we hang up our stockings," she said. "I'm so excited I can hardly wait."

Rosa Rabbit was not excited. She was hungry and lonely and sure nobody loved her.

Suddenly Brandon burst in. "Know what, Rosa Rabbit? It's snowing again. It's almost a blizzard!"

"Rosa probably doesn't remember what snow is," his sister said.

Brandon lifted Rosa out of her cage. He held her tight and ran back out into the winter dusk. He put her down gently in a stretch of fresh snow.

"How do you like the snow, Rosa?" he asked.

Just then his mother called, "Brandon, telephone!"

"I'm coming!" he yelled as he raced for the house.

Rosa waited and waited for him to come back. A gust of wind sent a burst of snowflakes right into her eyes.

When Brandon still did not come, she tried to follow his footprints, but it was dark and she could not see them any longer.

She was lost.

"Fluff up your feathers," said a small, clear voice.

Rosa gazed at the little bird.

"I don't have feathers," she said through chattering teeth.

"Maybe we can help," cheeped the bird. A flock of tiny chickadees flew down to her. They fluffed up their down to make a soft, busy blanket against the biting wind.

One hopped up between Rosa's soft ears and asked if that helped. Rosa nodded . . . but she was still shivering.

"Look who's here," peeped another of the birds.

Rosa lifted her head and peered through the swarming snowflakes. A creature with a tall tail appeared and dropped something right in front of her.

The chickadees twittered.

The squirrel went behind Rosa and gave her a push. Rosa jumped forward, and her ice-cold front paws landed on something. She moved around until she could get all four paws onto it.

The chickadees tumbled off her back and whirred up in a cloud of wings.

Rosa knew that mitt. It was Brandon's. She almost smiled as she settled onto the wonderful warmth of wool.

"Thanks," she mumbled to the squirrel, but all around her, the snow deepened.

"I'll get you something to eat," said a loud voice.

A raccoon waddled across to a tall, white shape nearby. He scrambled up it and came back with a carrot. He dropped it right in front of Rosa.

"I think it's supposed to be a nose," he said.

Rosa bit into the carrot. Never before had any food tasted so delicious.

"She really likes it," the raccoon boasted.

"We can see that, buddy," snapped a mouse, peering up with longing.

Rosa knew how it felt to be hungry. Every so often, Brandon forgot to feed her. She rolled the last little bit of carrot away with her nose and watched the mouse pounce upon it. For a moment, she felt almost warm.

Rosa Rabbit stared around at her new friends.

"I thought wild animals ate each other," she said.

"Not on this night," said a voice from a tree branch high above. "Even tasty little morsels like you are safe tonight."

"It's a hawk," cheeped the chickadee, trying to sound brave.

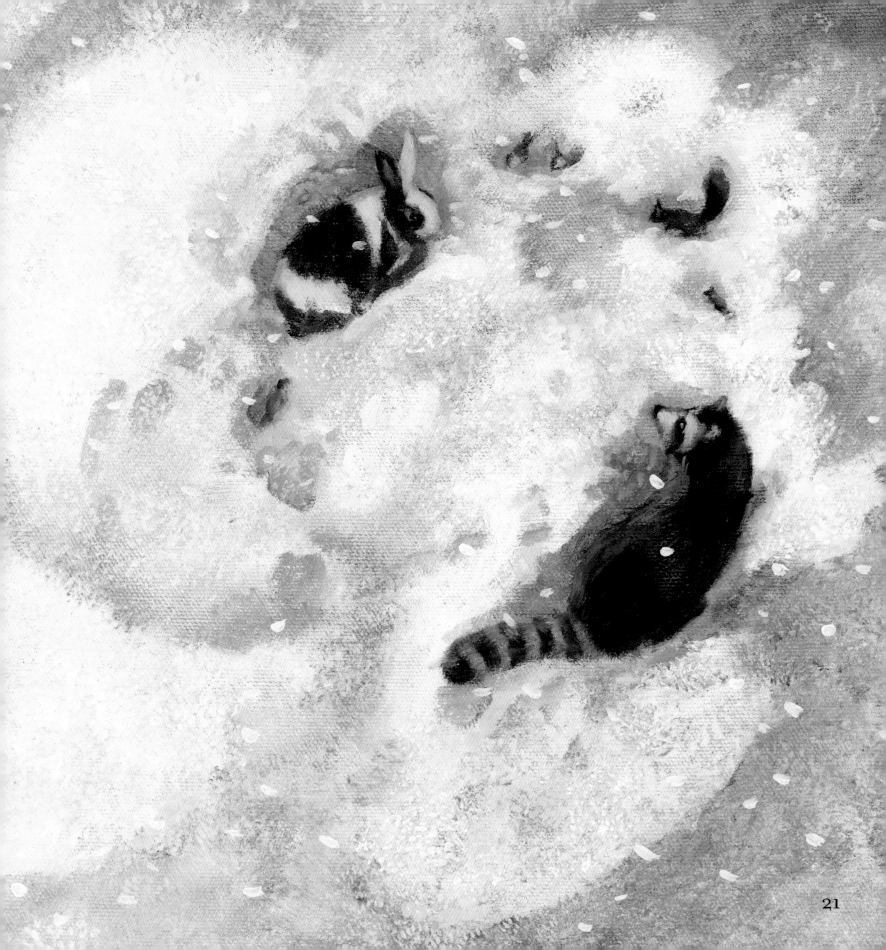

Rosa gazed up into the shadowy branches and remembered the Christmas tree in the warm house. Far away, someone was calling.

"I must go home," she said. "My boy will be in trouble." She stared into the darkness and trembled. "But I don't know where home is."

"You need to turn around," the hawk said. "I can guide you. I know where your boy lives."

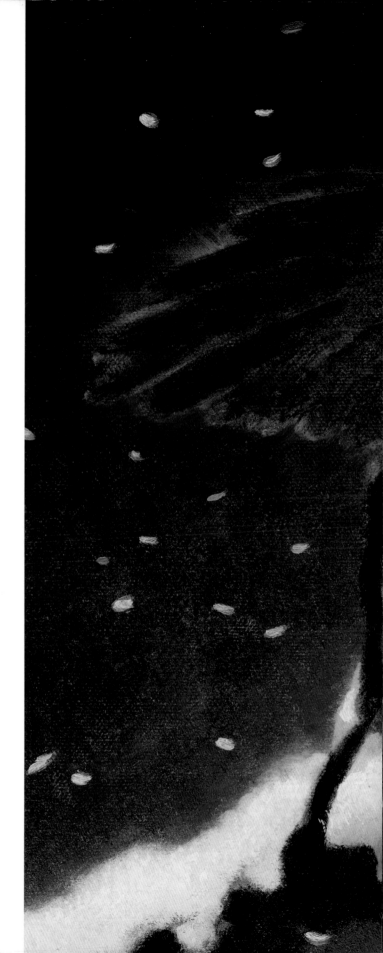

Rosa tried to move forward. But her paws felt stiff, in spite of the mitten's warmth, and the snow was so deep.

"I'm stuck," she whimpered.

"Don't be silly. You can hop," said the mouse.

"He's right," said the raccoon. "Be brave."

Then Rosa remembered Brandon shouting, "She's better than perfect."

"I *can*," she told herself, and she hopped with all her might.

As she sprang out of the snow, the hawk swooped down and flew ahead. The others followed after him. Soon they were in front of the house.

Brandon was just coming out the door.

Rosa gazed up at him. Then she looked back at all the creatures who had helped her when she was lost and afraid. "Thank you, everyone," she said.

As they scampered and flew away, she hopped up the porch steps and thumped with her hind foot.

Brandon looked down and saw her. For one moment he stared at her, not believing his eyes. Then he leaped forward and lifted her into his arms.

"Oh, Rosa, when I couldn't find you, I thought I'd lost you forever," Brandon cried.

She could have bitten him then, but she did not think of it. His arms were warm and she snuggled close. He did not need to tell her who loved Rosa Rabbit.

She knew.